How the Leopard Got Its Spots

3 TALES FROM AROUND THE WORLD

By Justine and Ron Fontes

Illustrated by Keiko Motoyama

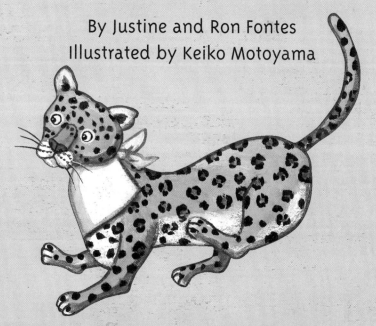

A GOLDEN BOOK • NEW YORK

Golden Books Publishing Company, Inc., New York, New York 10106

© 1999 Golden Books Publishing Company, Inc. All rights reserved. Printed in the U.S.A. No part of this book may be reproduced or copied in any form without written permission from the publisher. GOLDEN BOOKS®, A GOLDEN BOOK®, A LITTLE GOLDEN STORYBOOK®, G DESIGN®, and the distinctive gold spine are trademarks of Golden Books Publishing Company, Inc. Library of Congress Catalog Card Number: 99-64246   ISBN:0-307-16038-6
A MCMXCIX   First Edition 1999

We'd be happy to answer your questions and hear your comments. Please call us toll free at 1-888-READ-2-ME (1-888-732-3263). Hours: 8 AM—8 PM EST, weekdays. US and Canada only.

Greetings! I am Professor Polka—expert in the history of dots and spots and related topics. For years and years, people have been trying to figure out how the leopard got its spots. They've come up with some wild stories. Here are a few:

One tale from East Africa says that two lion cubs, let's call them Burt and Giggles, once watched some humans decorating their faces and bodies with paint.

"That looks like fun!" Giggles said.

Burt agreed.

As soon as the humans left, the cubs started painting each other. Giggles used his paws to put black spots all over Burt. Then it was Burt's turn to paint Giggles.

But before Burt could finish putting spots on his
brother, they heard the humans coming back. Burt was
so scared, he accidentally spilled the pot of paint over
Giggles's head!

The cubs quickly ran home to their cozy lion cave.
But the mother lion would not let them in.

"You are not lions!" she roared.

And, in fact, Mom was right! The half-black Giggles
had become the first hyena. And Burt, with his
gorgeous spots, had become the very first leopard.

Here is another story. This one is by the great British writer, Rudyard Kipling. According to Kipling, the Sandy Leopard was so good at hunting in the Sandy Savanna that he scared off the Sandy Wildebeest, the Sandy Zebra, and the Sandy Giraffe.

That is when the Sandy Leopard became the Hungry Sandy Leopard!

His former meals had fled to the Dark, Stripy, Splotchy Forest where they hid under the trees and bushes. After awhile, the sun, which peeked through the leaves and twigs and around the shadows, darkened the animals' skin in certain places.

The Sandy Wildebeest, the Sandy Zebra, and the Sandy Giraffe became the Dark Wildebeest, the Stripy Zebra, and the Splotchy Giraffe.

When the Hungry Sandy Leopard came into the
forest for dinner, he couldn't see any of the animals.
Their stripes and splotches helped them blend right
into their surroundings.

The Sandy Leopard discovered their trick and soon realized he needed to blend in, too, or else he could easily become someone else's dinner!

And that is how Kipling thinks the leopard got its spots.

Here's my very own theory:

   One day, a very long time ago, the first animals held a beauty contest. The slinky Lady Leopard was sure she would win—until she saw the fancy coats of the other contestants. How could her plain coat compete against such stylish stripes or gorgeous splotches, she wondered?

Then she saw one of the stage crew carrying a bucket of paint. The rest, as they say, is history.

Once Lady Leopard won the beauty contest, the other leopards followed the trend and added spots to their coats as well.

But that is just one more story about how the leopard got its spots. The truth is . . .

you'll have to keep wondering! Because nobody really knows how the leopard got its spots.
How do YOU think it happened?

LEOPARD FACTS

One thing we do know is that leopards are really cool animals. Here are some true fun facts about them:

SPOTS, SPOTS, AND MORE SPOTS

Leopards have spots all over their bodies, from their nose to their toes, and even on the end of their long tail. The only place leopards don't have spots is inside their ears.

TREE CLIMBERS

If you want to find a leopard, you should first look for a tree. Leopards like to lounge in trees during the day and hunt at night. And they always climb down a tree head first.

HOME SWEET HOME

Leopards live in almost every area of the African continent, except the Sahara Desert region. They can also be found in parts of Asia and the Middle East.

SEPARATED AT BIRTH

For a long time scientists thought spotted leopards and black panthers were separate species. Now they know that panthers are really just very dark leopards, born in the same litter as regular leopards. In bright sunlight, you can see that black panthers actually have darker spots in the same pattern as their sandy siblings.